The Magic School Bus
Inside the Human Body

By Joanna Cole   Illustrated by Bruce Degen

SCHOLASTIC INC.

New York Toronto London Auckland Sydney

The author and illustrator wish to thank Dr. Arnold J. Capute,
Associate Professor of Pediatrics, Director, Division of Child Development,
Johns Hopkins University School of Medicine, for his help in preparing this book.

ISBN 0-590-41427-5

20 19   2 3 4 5/9

Printed in the U.S.A.   08

The very next day, The Friz made us do an experiment on our own bodies.

Then she announced that we were going on a class trip to the science museum. We were going to see an exhibit about how our bodies get energy from the food we eat.

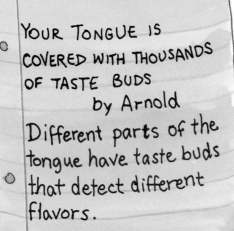

The trip started out like any other trip.
We rode to the museum
in the old school bus.
Along the way,
we stopped at a park for lunch.

When it was time to go,
everyone got back on the bus—
everyone but Arnold.
He was still at the picnic table,
daydreaming and eating
a bag of Cheesie-Weesies.

WHEN YOU EAT, YOUR BODY DIGESTS THE FOOD SO YOUR CELLS CAN USE IT TO MAKE ENERGY.

YOUR BODY NEEDS GOOD FOOD
by Carmen
For high energy and good growing power eat lots of:

Fresh fruits and Vegetables

Milk and Milk products

Whole grain cereal and Pasta

Lean Meats, Fish, Poultry, AND eggs

AND NOT TOO MUCH JUNK FOOD!

A SCIENCE WORD
by Dorothy Ann

Digestion comes from a word that means to divide. When food is digested it is divided into smaller and smaller parts.

"Hurry up, Arnold!" called Ms. Frizzle. She reached for the ignition key, but instead she pushed a strange little button nearby.

At once, we started shrinking and spinning through the air.

From inside, we couldn't see what was happening. All we knew was that we landed suddenly...

and then we were going down a dark tunnel.
We had no idea where we were.
But, as usual, Ms. Frizzle knew.
She said we were inside a human body,
going down the esophagus—
the tube that leads from the throat
to the stomach.
Most of us were too upset
about leaving Arnold behind
to pay much attention.

WHERE'S ARNOLD?

HE GOT LEFT!

THAT'S WHAT HAPPENS WHEN YOU EAT JUNK FOOD!

I THOUGHT WE WERE GOING TO THE MUSEUM.

THERE'S BEEN A SLIGHT CHANGE OF PLANS... WE'RE BEING DIGESTED INSTEAD.

FOOD GOES TO YOUR STOMACH THROUGH THE ESOPHAGUS
by Wanda
The food does not just fall down. It is pushed along by muscle actions the way toothpaste is squeezed out of a tube. That's why you can swallow even when you are upside down.

MUSCLES SQUEEZE TO PUSH FOOD TO YOUR STOMACH

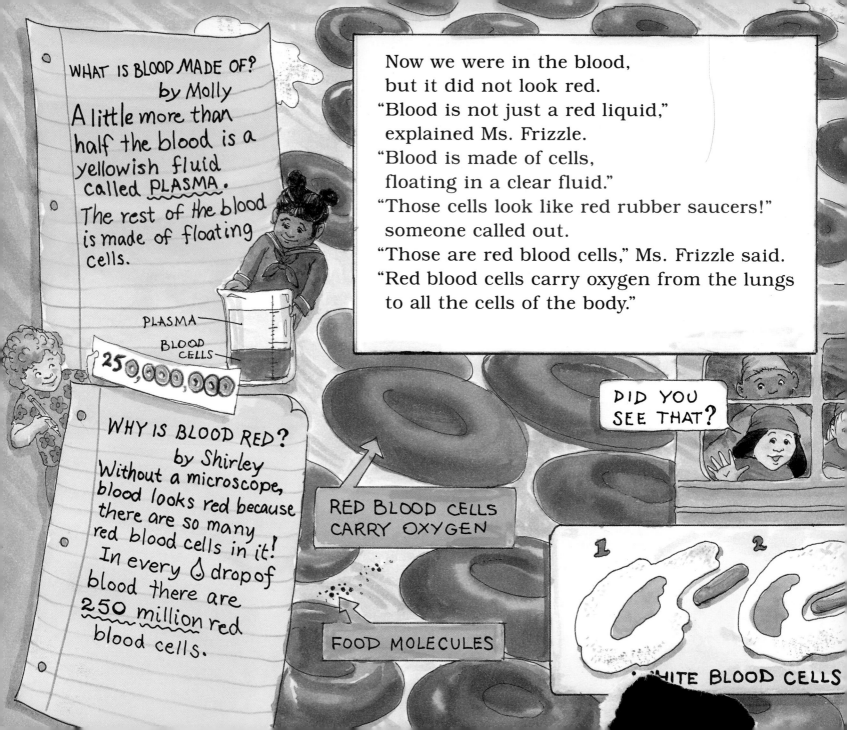

WHAT IS BLOOD MADE OF?
by Molly

A little more than half the blood is a yellowish fluid called PLASMA.
The rest of the blood is made of floating cells.

PLASMA

BLOOD CELLS

250,000,000

WHY IS BLOOD RED?
by Shirley

Without a microscope, blood looks red because there are so many red blood cells in it!
In every drop of blood there are 250 million red blood cells.

Now we were in the blood, but it did not look red.
"Blood is not just a red liquid," explained Ms. Frizzle.
"Blood is made of cells, floating in a clear fluid."
"Those cells look like red rubber saucers!" someone called out.
"Those are red blood cells," Ms. Frizzle said.
"Red blood cells carry oxygen from the lungs to all the cells of the body."

DID YOU SEE THAT?

RED BLOOD CELLS CARRY OXYGEN

FOOD MOLECULES

1   2

WHITE BLOOD CELLS

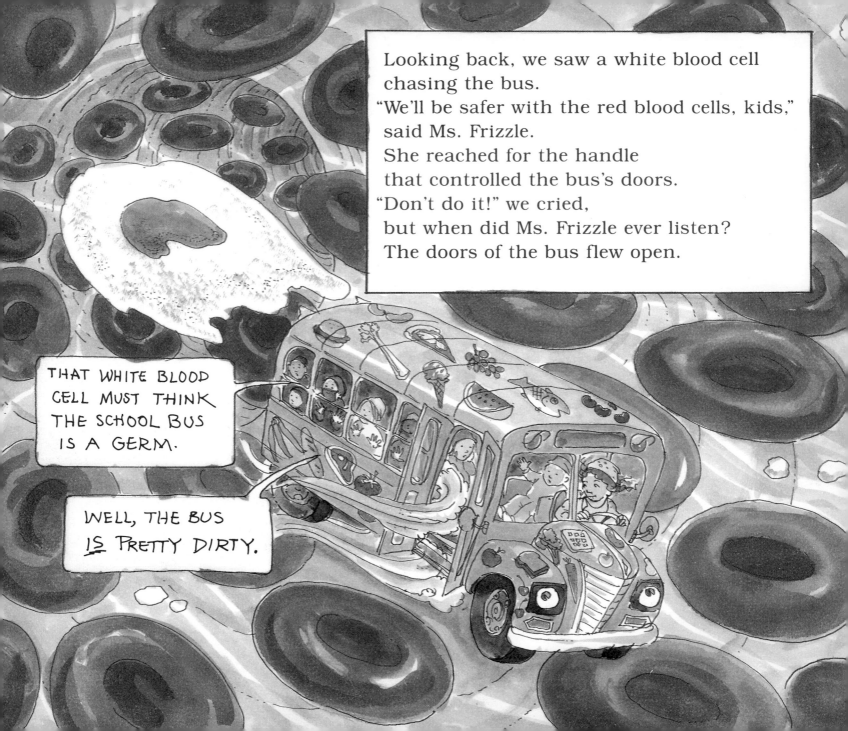

We were swept out of the bus
and into the bloodstream.
"Everybody hitch a ride!" called The Friz.
Each kid grabbed a red blood cell
as it went by.
Our last glimpse of the bus
was when it went into another blood vessel—
with the white blood cell right behind it!

BLOOD GOES ROUND
AND ROUND
by Michael
In less than a minute
your blood makes
a trip all around
your body.
This is called the
circulation of the
blood.

ONE MORE SCIENCE WORD
by Dorothy Ann
Circulate comes from
a word that means
"to circle". Blood
Circulates - circles -
all around your body.

From the lungs, our red blood cells
carried us back to the heart.
This time we were on the left side
of the heart—the side that pumps
fresh blood back to the body again.
"Kids, it looks as if these red
blood cells are on their way to
the brain," said Ms. Frizzle.

LOOK! WHEN THE
RED BLOOD CELLS
PICK UP OXYGEN, THEY
TURN BRIGHT RED.

FROM RIGHT LUNG

AIR SAC

When we reached the brain, we let go of our red blood cells and squeezed out of the blood vessel. It was hard to believe that this wrinkled gray blob was the control center of the body.

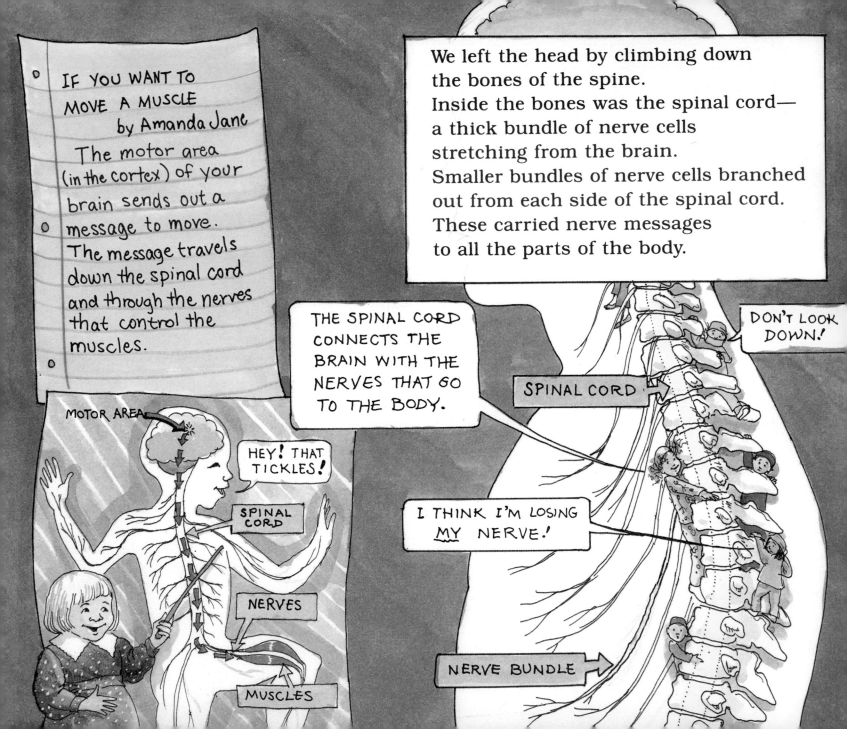

When we emerged from the bloodstream,
we were in a huge open space.
"Where are we?" asked a kid.
Ms. Frizzle explained,
"Children, this is the nasal cavity."
"The what?" we asked.
"The inside of the nose," said The Friz.
Suddenly, we heard a deafening noise.
It sounded like "Ah-aa-aa-ah!"

A tremendous blast of air
hit the bus full force.
We flew forward,
spinning around and around.

"Arnold!" we said, "the trip was *amazing!* You should have been there!"

THE KIDNEYS CLEAN YOUR BLOOD AND MAKE URINE.

THE BLADDER STORES URINE.

KIDNEYS

BLADDER

LIVER

STOMACH

THE LIVER STORES VITAMINS AND DESTROYS POISONS. IT ALSO MAKES BILE, A FLUID THAT HELPS DIGEST FATTY FOODS.

Back in the classroom, it was business as usual. Ms. Frizzle made us draw a chart of the human body for the bulletin board.

BLOOD VESSEL

NERVE

BONE

MUSCLE

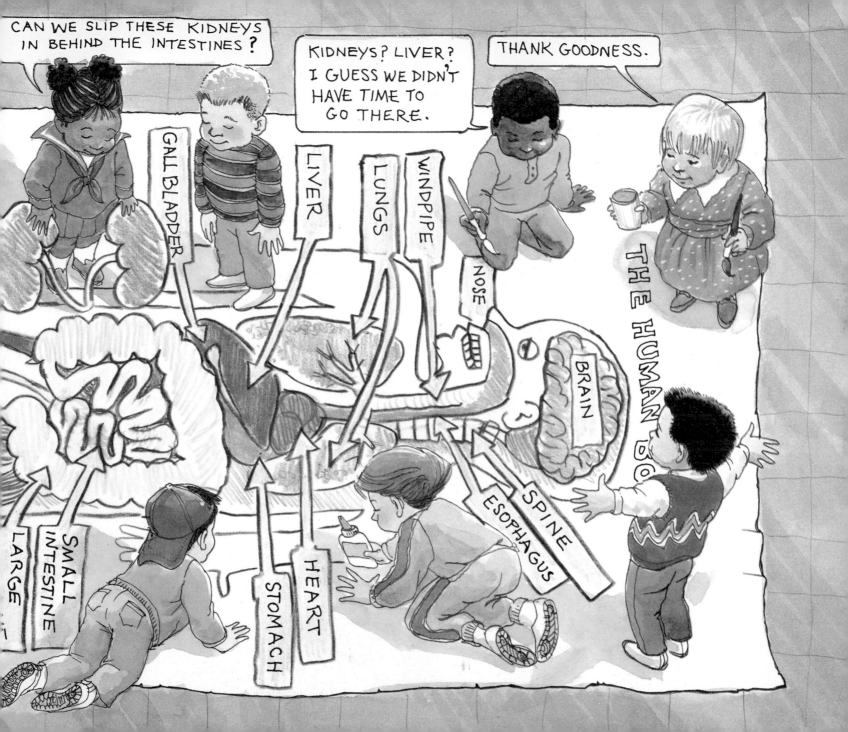

TRUE-OR-FALSE TEST

STOP! TAKE THIS TEST!
DO NOT WATCH T.V. ... YET.
DO NOT GET A SNACK ... YET.
DO NOT PLAY A VIDEO
GAME ... YET.

FIRST TAKE THIS TEST.

HOW TO:
Read the sentences below. Decide if each one is true or false. To see if you are correct, check the answers on the opposite page.

QUESTIONS:

1. A school bus can enter someone's body and kids can go on a tour. True or false?

2. Museums are boring. True or false?

3. Arnold should not have tried to get back to school by himself. True or false?

4. Children cannot breathe or talk when they are surrounded by a liquid. True or false?

5. If the children really were as small as cells, we couldn't see them without a microscope. True or false?

6. White blood cells actually chase and destroy disease germs. True or false?

7. Ms. Frizzle really knew where Arnold was the whole time. True or false?

ANSWERS:

1. False! That could not happen in real life. (Not even to Arnold.)

   But in this story the author had to make it happen. Otherwise, the book would have been about a trip to a museum, instead of a trip through the body.

2. False! Museums are interesting and fun. But they are not as weird and gross as actually going inside a human body.

3. True! In real life, it would have been safer if Arnold had found a police officer to help.

4. True. If children were *really* inside a blood vessel, they would drown. It must have been magic.

5. True! The pictures in this book show the cells and the children greatly enlarged.

6. True! As unbelievable as it seems, real white blood cells actually behave just like the ones in this book. They even squeeze through the cells of blood vessel walls to capture germs in your organs and tissues.

7. Probably true. No one is absolutely sure, but most people think Ms. Frizzle knows *everything.*

PLEASE DO NOT WRITE IN THIS BOOK.

THANK YOU.